Janie's N

Janie's New Legs

*To Natalie —
Enjoy this
story of friendship!
Diana*

Diana Tuorto

2008

Janie's New Legs

TABLE OF CONTENTS

This book is dedicated to my horses, Luna and Classy, and my cats, Norm, Daisy, Flash, and Newton, who continue to show me that love and friendship can conquer all obstacles.

"In riding a horse, we borrow freedom."

—Helen Thompson

"By the time Ken reached Flicka in the morning, she...was standing broadside to the level sunlight, gathering in every ultraviolet ray, every infrared, for the healing and the recreation her battered body needed."

—Mary O'Hara, from My Friend Flicka

*"I was very much troubled, and I put my nose up to hers, but I could say nothing to comfort her. I think she was pleased to see me, for she said,
'You are the only friend I ever had.'"*

—Anna Sewell, from Black Beauty

Chapter 1

New Beginning

My life truly began when I was seven years old at Mrs. Johnson's farm. It was a large, old estate with a long, stone driveway, lined by tall pine trees. A brown stable stood on one side of a wide pasture, which was covered by wet snow. On the other side of the pasture was a small orchard. At the top of the driveway stood a huge farmhouse, white with dark green trim and decorated with streams of pine needles. I looked out of the trailer window, my legs shaking, as the door swung open.

"So, is this the new pony you've promised us?" said the gray-haired woman.

"You betcha." said Nancy, the blond lady who had taken care of me at my last home. "Mrs. Johnson, this is Silver Lining, but of course we just call him Silver."

Nancy backed me slowly out of the trailer, and Mrs. Johnson immediately kissed my gray muzzle.

"He's beautiful," said Mrs. Johnson. "How could anyone have hurt this poor animal?"

"I agree," said Nancy. "When we got Silver, he was just a bag of bones with overgrown hooves and bruises everywhere. It's taken him a while to trust people, but he's made amazing progress. I know he'll have a wonderful new home with you now! I'm so glad you could take him."

"Oh, the kids will love him!" said the gray-haired woman. "And we'll make sure he keeps his plump figure for the rest of his days."

I turned to my side and stared at my belly. I didn't think I looked *that* plump...

"Well, speaking of, it's time for dinner!" said Mrs. Johnson. "Thanks again, Nancy. We'll let you know how he's settling in."

"Take care." said Nancy, as she locked the trailer door and drove off.

As soon as I heard "dinner," which at my previous home meant a bucket of grain, I didn't hesitate to follow Mrs. Johnson. She led me down the stone driveway towards a stable. As we walked inside, I could see three horses, two in the left row of stalls and one on the right, their eyes looking me over curiously. Mrs. Johnson walked me into a stall at the end of the stable and I was given hay and a bucket of sweet grain, which was my favorite.

Once I finished eating, I began to look over the other horses. In the stall next to me was an old, leopard-spotted Appaloosa, lying in his bedding and snoring loudly. I was so excited to learn more about my new home that I gave a hard kick to the wall between us. The Appaloosa jumped right to his feet, his head knocking into the metal hayrack above him.

"Ouucccch!" the horse yelled. "What was that for?!"

"Sorry!" I said, turning my eyes downward. "My name is Silver. I just got here, so I'm not sure what to expect..."

"The name's Pepper, and I saw you arrive," said the Appaloosa. "And you should know better than to wake up an old man after his dinner. You don't look this good at my age by staying up all night, you know? I have to work tomorrow."

"I didn't realize. What kind of work?" I said.

"Mrs. Johnson retired a few years ago, after her husband died," said the spotted horse. "She started a program at the farm for special children. Most of them can't walk or have other problems. They're a nice bunch of kids and are more appreciative of us than the other children that I've met. I guess you'd be that way too if the only time you could walk was riding on horseback. And they bring us the best treats you've ever tasted."

My mouth began to water.

"That sounds great! I've never worked with children before, but I think I'll like it," I said.

"Sure you will," said the Appaloosa. "This is the best job I've ever had. But, like I said, I need to get some rest now. I'll talk to you more in the morning."

"No problem. Thanks for filling me in!" I said.

I looked around to see if any other horses were interested in talking, but the only sounds were the rattling of buckets and Pepper's snoring. I wondered what the children would be like. As much as I liked the idea of working with kids, I was a little afraid of them. From what I'd seen, from a distance, they were small and full of energy. You never knew what to expect. But, Pepper had assured me that these children were different. I tried to relax and buried my head back into my hay.

Before I knew it, the sun was streaming through the stable windows and I awoke to the sound of crows calling outside. Pepper, the old Appaloosa, was already awake and munching on some hay, so I moved over to speak with him.

"Sorry how I acted last night," said Pepper. "I can be a cranky old gelding when I don't get my rest. I'm just lucky these old bones have lasted as long as they have. Thirty years of work can make a horse pretty tired."

"You're HOW old?" I gasped.

"Don't act so surprised." Pepper said, with a laugh. "Horses live longer everyday. Why, I heard some horse lived to be in his late forties once, and, at the rate I'm going, I might as well hold out a little longer to break the record. That's why it's so important that I get my rest."

"I guess so..." I said.

"So, did you meet either of the others during the evening?" Pepper asked.

"Well, no...no one else seemed too interested in speaking to me," I said.

"Nonsense!" Pepper stated. "You just have to get their attention."

Pepper held his breath and clamped his lips tightly together. He lifted his head high above the stall door and let out a loud whinny. By the time he was done, the two other horses in the stable were awake, and angry. A voice called out from across the stable.

"What do you want, old horse?" shouted a bay mare. "Don't you EVER sleep late?"

"That's Morning Star," said Pepper. "Next to me, she is the crankiest horse on the farm."

"Shut up NOW, Pepper!" yelled the mare, who had a large white star marking on her forehead.

"See what I mean..." said the gelding.

I laughed and tried to fill my mouth with hay at the same time.

"Can't you ever be quiet, Pep?" shouted a short chestnut and white paint. "Hey, who's the peewee? Is he replacing Coco?"

"Yes, Patches, he is," said Pepper. "This is our new friend, Silver. He's going to be staying with us from now on."

"Where are you from, Silver? Another rescue?" asked Star.

I lowered my head.

"I guess that's what you call it, and I'm really grateful to be here now," I answered. "Who's Coco?"

"Oh, Coco was a nice fella, a short pony, like yourself," Pepper explained. "He was getting close to forty years old, and his heart gave out one night. He was a favorite with the young children, but I'm sure they're going to love you too. And don't listen to Star...she can be a snob and thinks rescues aren't as good. And Patches is barely taller than you, so he can't call you silly names, like peewee. Besides, I'm boss of this herd, so you won't catch either of them giving you a hard time again."

I barely knew him, but I liked Pepper tremendously. I was sure I could always call that old gelding my friend.

Chapter 2

My First Rider

After we finished our morning hay and grain, the birds' chirping was silenced by the sound of tires scraping up the stone driveway. The stable door was shut tightly, so I couldn't see, but it sounded like cars arriving. Soon, the stable door rolled open, and Mrs. Johnson walked down the row of stalls, giving each of us a carrot.

"Good morning, Silver!" Mrs. Johnson said, patting my neck. "How would you like to go to work today? Why don't we see who would like to ride you?"

Mrs. Johnson fastened a green halter on my face and led me to a set of crossties, or ropes on either side of me. Three children appeared in the stable, two standing on their own, and one little boy in a metal seat with wheels, which I learned was called a wheelchair. Each one, with the help of their mother or father, began pulling out saddles and other riding equipment from a separate room. Then, I saw a tiny girl roll into the stable, sitting tall in a wheelchair and wearing a purple sweater. Her long, red hair was braided tightly. Her mother stood behind her, holding onto the handles.

"Mom, I can do it myself," said the girl, her red hands forcefully pushing the wheels along the stable aisle.

"Alright, sweetie, I'll go say hello to Mrs. Johnson. Call me if you need anything," said her mother.

The girl and I locked eyes for a moment and stared at each other. To me, her eyes felt sad, even scared, but with a certain strength underneath them. I could tell that like me, she felt beaten, but like me, she wasn't going to lie down and give in.

The girl continued to rolled her wheelchair down the aisle and stopped right in front of me. I had never seen this type of metal device before, especially up close, so I snorted and pulled away.

"Don't worry, I'm not afraid of you," said the girl. "And I won't hurt you."

She extended her arm towards me. I hesitated at first, but eventually reached out and nuzzled her small hand, which smelled like lavender. The girl's warm fingers opened to reveal a carrot. I gently took it in my mouth.

"Hi pretty boy," the girl whispered. "I'm Janie."

Janie sat there, looking me over with a smile on her face. Her lonely, blue eyes began to light up. I nuzzled her soft hair as she gently untangled my gray mane with her fingers. Mrs. Johnson soon approached us.

"Janie, I think there's someone who wants to see you," said Mrs. Johnson.

"Do I have to ride Star today, Mrs. Johnson?" Janie asked.

"You mean you don't want to ride her?" said Janie's mother. "You've been riding Star for a year!"

"I know…but this one's nice, too," said the shy girl. "How about him?"

"That's fine." said Mrs. Johnson. "I was planning on having Silver work with one of the other kids, but Star is great with anyone. Janie, you can tack Silver up if you want. His saddle and bridle are on the rack."

Janie's eyes and smile grew wide and, for the first time in my life, I felt instantly loved. The tiny girl wheeled herself over to my side and gently brushed me. I examined the metal chair closely and finally determined that it would not eat me. Her mother held up each of my legs while Janie cleaned my hooves and then fixed the saddle on my back. Janie was about to hand her mother the bridle, but I lowered my head right to her, scooping the bit into my mouth and allowing her to fix the device on my face.

I began to wonder what life must be like not being able to use your legs. All of the children added extra straps and equipment to their saddles, which I had never seen. Some, like Janie, had metal objects, that I later heard called braces, on their legs, back, or necks. But no matter what, all of the children were smiling and happily tending to their horses, and I felt lucky to be working with Janie.

I was tacked up within a few minutes, then Janie's mother lifted the girl into the saddle. She was so light that I could hardly feel the weight of her. Ahead of us were Pepper and his rider, Mark, a thin, eleven year-old boy. Pepper would later tell me that Mark was frequently sick and had a rare illness that none of us could understand. Pepper said it kept him young trying to make Mark laugh. Whenever he saw the boy nearby, Pepper would lift his head high and nicker to him. Mark was always smiling around Pepper.

Pepper, Star, Patches, and I were led out of the stable by our riders. We headed towards the white farmhouse into a small, sandy paddock, as the snow beneath our hooves began to melt. Each horse, myself included, had two helpers walking along with us—one person would lead the horse, and the other attended to the rider. Janie and I walked with Heidi and Sarah, whom I learned were Mrs. Johnson's twin teenage daughters. I could only tell them apart by their clothes as both girls had bold green eyes and short, blond hair.

"How do you like him, Janie?" asked Sarah, who was walking close to my side.

"He's great!" Janie replied, throwing her arms in the air for a moment. "He's the most beautiful horse in the world."

"Quiet, Janie!" said Heidi, smiling widely. "If the other horses hear that, they might get jealous!"

The three girls laughed as we walked around the paddock, following Pepper. Janie praised me during the ride and didn't pull on the reins too hard, as my former owner did. Near the end of our ride, Janie asked if she could lead me herself, without Heidi, but with Sarah holding her in the saddle. Heidi agreed and let go of my reins as we walked along.

"Where did you find him?" Janie asked. "He looks like a show pony."

"Actually, we adopted him from the Avery's farm," said Sarah.

"The Avery's?" Janie said. "Isn't that the farm for rescue horses?"

"That's right," said Sarah. "A bad man owned Silver and didn't treat him well at all. When Heidi and I first saw him, he was so skinny. Over the past year, he's recovered, so we decided to adopt him."

I didn't like to think about my former owner, but sometimes I couldn't help but remember. He had bought me as a colt, claiming I was for his daughter. When I arrived at his home, I learned there was no daughter, and most of my time I was left locked in a dark shed with little hay or water. When I did come out, it was only to work, riding the steep trails nearby with the heavy man on my back. Since I couldn't go as fast as he liked, he would hit me with a crop, or riding whip. This went on for what seemed like eternity, but finally the family next door told the Avery's and they saved me.

"How could somebody hurt Silver?" cried Janie. "He's so sweet. Is he all right now?"

"Oh yeah, don't worry," said Heidi. "He's all better. Silver just needs some TLC. To be honest, I'm surprised he's so trusting after what happened to him."

"Don't worry, Silver," said Janie, patting my neck. "I'll come visit you all the time and bring you yummy treats. No one will ever hurt you again, now that you're my friend."

Chapter 3

A Special Friend

After our ride, Janie hooked me to a pair of crossties in the stable. She finished brushing me when Sarah walked over with a leadrope.

"Thanks, Janie. If you're all finished with Silver, I'm going to walk him out to the field," said Sarah.

"Can I walk him?" Janie asked. "I'll put him out in the field for you."

"Sure," Sarah said. "But please be careful of the others. Pepper likes to run out, if you give him the chance."

"I know. I will," said Janie.

The little girl wheeled herself with one hand and held my leadrope with the other. I walked carefully, trying to keep my legs clear of the wheelchair. We slowly moved towards the field's gate, on a thin area of cement, which allowed Janie to roll along more easily. It took several minutes to reach the field, but I didn't care. It was a few more precious minutes with my new friend.

"You're a good horse, Silver," said Janie, smiling. "I can't believe someone would hurt you. I promise, I'm only going to ride *you* from now on. I'll try to see you whenever I can, even if it's only once a week. I can't think of any place else I'd rather be. It's either here, or school, or..."

Janie paused and looked down at her thin legs.

"Or therapy," said the girl, in a faint whisper.

I looked at Janie's legs and wished they were strong and firm like mine. No matter how much my old owner had hurt me, I always had good, solid legs to carry me. I couldn't imagine being confined as she was.

Janie reached for the green gate and carefully led me inside. I nickered softly as Janie slipped off my halter and pushed herself out of the field. Her face looked blank and sunken as she left. She rolled herself down the path towards her mother's car, never once looking up from her chair. At that moment, I swore to always treat Janie as special as she treated me. I would pay extra attention to her. I now felt it was my purpose to make that little girl smile and be happy.

As Janie rolled away, I followed her, whinnying. As she watched me from the car window, her eyes looked blank, but she managed to flash a small smile at me and soon disappeared from sight. Suddenly, I could hear Pepper, Star, and Patches nickering for me to come over. I carefully trudged through the diminishing snow to the tree line, where they stood.

"I see you've made friends with Janie," said Star. "She's such a sweet girl, but incredibly quiet and distant. I've been riding with her since she started coming to the farm, but I barely know her."

"She's just shy," stated Pepper. "Janie's not like a lot of the other kids. She actually used to walk, until..."

Pepper stopped and looked over at Star. Both had somber expressions.

"What?" I asked. "Until what?"

"Janie was in a car accident." Pepper said. "Mrs. Johnson told Sarah the story once. She was five, I think, and driving with her father down a road. Another car hit them. Since then, Janie's been paralyzed, almost completely, from the waist down. She barely feels anything in those legs. They're useless now."

"What happened to her father?" I asked.

Pepper was silent, so Star spoke up:

"I heard that he passed away."

"How horrible!" I said, turning my head away.

"It is," said Star. "I guess that's why Janie keeps to herself. Don't be hurt if she doesn't come around with you, either. It's just her way. It can't be easy for her to make friends, human or otherwise."

I had always pitied myself, thinking that no one else's past could've possibly been worse than my own. How wrong I was. Still, I hoped that I could reach that lonely little girl, even more than I already had. If the rescue farm workers could get through to me, I could get through to Janie. It would take time.

The next morning, after a long, restful sleep, I woke up to find a full bucket of grain and few flakes of hay in my stall. Pepper was already loudly munching his oats.

"So, what's going on today, Pep?" I asked.

The spotted face lifted out of his bucket, letting tiny grain morsels escape from his droopy lips.

"Well," said Pepper, while chewing his food. "I just heard Mrs. Johnson say that Mark had to cancel his lesson. He's not feeling well. However, it appears that Janie's coming out to ride you again today."

"Really?" I said, surprised. "She said she might only be able to visit once a week."

"Well, she was like that with Star," said Pepper. "But after yesterday, it appears that you're her favorite horse, Silver. You might find that little girl's heart, after all."

Chapter 4

Learning To Walk

I tried to eat my grain, but I was too excited to stand still, so I paced around my stall after every gulp. I kept looking at the stable door, searching for the little girl's face.

Soon, Heidi, Sarah, and Mrs. Johnson appeared. They put warmer blankets on Pepper, Star, and Patches and slowly led them out of the stable.

"Looks like you're the only one with a lesson today, Silver," Patches said. "Have fun!"

I snorted at Patches and finished my grain. The stable was now empty. Moments went by and there was no sign of Janie. Finally, I heard the familiar roar of a car engine from outside. Soon afterwards, the small girl rolled down the stable aisle, her smile as wide and inviting as ever. She pulled something red from her pocket.

"Here's an apple, Silver!" Janie said. "I made Mom stop at the store for one."

I quickly swallowed the apple.

Janie's mom appeared in the stable and led me from my stall, as Janie sang to me.

"Silver is the best-est horse...the great-est hooorse there ever was!"

After a good brushing and tacking me up, Janie's mother lifted her into the saddle and helped hold her there.

"Riding is going to strengthen my legs, Mom," said Janie, proudly. "You'll see. Someday, I'm going to walk as well as Silver."

Janie's mother patted my neck softly as we headed along the stone path. I glanced at the pasture where Pepper and my stablemates were. The three horses nickered and began to chase each other, as snow and dirt, kicked up by their hooves, flew behind them.

Other than the horses running, it was extremely quiet. The sky was gray and eerily absent of birds singing.

"Janie, I'm going up to the house," said her mother. "Mrs. Johnson must have forgotten about the lesson. You can stay here with Silver, if you trust him."

"Mom, this isn't a mustang; it's Silver!" Janie said, with a laugh. "He's even safer than Scruffy. I'll be fine. We'll wait here."

Janie's mother smiled and headed towards the farmhouse. I stood there quietly, but after a moment Janie began to cluck, trying to urge me forward. I knew we weren't supposed to go anywhere, but I followed Janie's commands. The girl picked up the reins and led me into the riding paddock at a steady walk. Janie began to laugh and I followed her commands through her arms and the reins. When her hands on the reins guided me left, I went left, and so on.

Janie continued to urge me forward. I picked up a very slow trot, as she grabbed some of my long mane to keep her balance. Suddenly, we came around the ring to see Mrs. Johnson and Janie's mother standing there, and neither looked pleased.

"Janie! What do you think you're doing?!" shouted her mother.

"I'm riding a horse," Janie said. "What does it look like? I trotted *alone* for once. Did you see?!"

"You could've fallen and killed yourself!" screamed Janie's mother. "Come on, get off this pony, right now! We're going home."

"No!" shouted Janie. "I have a lesson, and I'm staying here."

"Don't worry, Mrs. Cannon." said Mrs. Johnson calmly. "I know it's scary, but Janie's fine with Silver. He was the gentlest pony Heidi and Sarah could find on the rescue farm, and Janie's taken a lot of lessons. Maybe we should give her some time to work with Silver on her own, but under supervision, of course. Is that all right with both of you?"

"Yes! Please?" said Janie.

"Well...all right," stated Janie's mother. "But only under supervision."

After that, Janie and I had our lesson with Mrs. Johnson. Over time, I would learn to respond to voice and hand signals in addition to reins, as that was all Janie could use to direct me.

As our lesson ended, Janie walked me over to Mrs. Johnson, who lifted her out of the saddle. The girl smiled so happily that I felt warm all over, in spite of the snow and wind surrounding us.

"I love riding with Silver. It's like having a new set of legs, Mom!"

And that's when I became Janie's New Legs...

Chapter 5

Pepper

One morning, when it was particularly cold and snowy, Mrs. Johnson left us all in our stalls with extra grain and hay. Since we didn't have a lot of ways to pass the time, other than eating or sleeping, I asked Pepper to tell me about his long life.

"There isn't too much to tell," said the old Appaloosa. "I was never a racehorse or a show horse, or anything exciting. I remember growing up on a large farm. When I was six months old, I was weaned from my mother and sold to a family who had visited me since I was born. They had a small backyard, but it had enough grass to keep me fat and happy."

"I know all about being fat..." I said.

"Yes, well, the mother apparently had raised foals before, so I was very well-cared for, and the two children, a boy and girl, treated me like a puppy. For my first two years, I was spoiled. I grazed around the yard all day until the children came home. They would each grab a brush and groom both sides of me, until my spots were jet black and my white coat was shining."

"Then, when I was about two years old," Pepper continued, "The mother began to train me. She put me on a lunge line, a long leadrope so I could move freely, and then fitted me with a saddle and bridle. I still remember how strange the cold bit felt, but other than tossing my head and stomping my foot a few times, I didn't fight. The woman was very light, so having her ride me was a pleasure. They even trusted me enough to ride with the children. Some days, I would be taken out on the trails, near the house, with both children. When their friends came over, I gave everyone pony rides, and everyone loved me."

"So," I interrupted. "Why aren't you with them now?"

"They went away," sighed Pepper. "Like all children do. After many seasons together, the girl and boy moved away. Once they left, the mother felt bad that I was alone so much and sold me to Mrs. Johnson, back when her husband was still alive. I was their riding horse, then Heidi and Sarah's, before they started this program for disabled children. I hate to admit it, but, while I enjoy being here on the farm, I still get lonely sometimes thinking about my old family."

"Well, at least you have Mark now, right?" I said.

"Yes," Pepper stated. "But Mark gets sick, very sick. I'm not sure how much longer he can keep riding. I thought riding might make him better, but lately he's been home more often. He's getting too weak to even visit. If I don't have him around, what else do I have to look forward to?"

I didn't know how to respond to Pepper. I had never formed an attachment to someone as Pepper had, so I didn't mind being alone. But in just a few days with Janie, I was starting to see how easy it was to bond with a human, and, through Pepper, how devastating it would be when it was gone.

Chapter 6

A Walk In The Woods

The next morning came and with it, a new group of small children eager for a ride. One little girl braided Patches' mane, while two other girls groomed Star and Pepper. I patiently stood in my stall when I noticed Janie approaching. In her hands was a black halter with something shiny gleaming from one of the side straps.

"Look Silver, there's your name!" said Janie proudly. "Mom let me buy this halter as a Christmas present for you! Now everyone will know it's yours. Let me put it on you."

I lowered my head as Janie fastened on the halter. Pepper and Star whinnied their approval, and it was soft and comfortable. I had never been given something like this before, and it made me feel very special.

After the usual grooming, Heidi boosted Janie into the saddle and led us outside.

"It's really getting cold out there," said Heidi. "Are you sure you're up for the ride?"

"You bet!" Janie replied. "We'll ride for just a little while."

As Janie and I left the stable, a strong wind forced me to lower my head and dig in with my hooves. Janie urged me forward with a pat.

"Janie! I need to speak to your mother for a second, so why don't you and Silver head up to the paddock? We'll be there in five minutes…" said Heidi.

Snow began to fall and the harsh wind made my fur stand up on end. Once Heidi was back inside the stable, Janie said, "walk on, Silver." I noticed she was leading me away from the paddock and towards the barren orchard.

Under Janie's direction, I walked down the small hill that led us into the orchard. She urged me on, and I could see we were heading towards the forest. I hesitated, knowing we shouldn't be going this way.

"Let's go, Silver," said Janie. "It's fine. Trot on, boy."

I didn't want to disappoint Janie, so I picked up a trot and continued on into the woods.

The trees soon grew too thick to trot ahead, so I slowed to a walk and proceeded carefully. After several moments, we were deep in the forest, weaving our way through tall pine and locust trees. Soon, I began to hear the sound of laughter and voices ahead. I immediately felt uneasy.

"Come on, Silver," said Janie. "Let's walk up a little further and then we'll turn back. I hate always riding in that ring. It's nicer out here."

Suddenly, three boys jumped down from a tree's branches. A stocky one ran up and grabbed the reins from underneath my neck. A taller boy walked over to Janie.

"What are you doing here? You're trespassing," said the stocky, brown-haired boy. "This is our hideout. Get out of here."

"Um, sorry..." Janie stammered. "I just wanted to ride my horse out here, but I'll leave."

"Wait," said the tall, blond-haired boy. "I want to ride him."

"I can't get off by myself," said Janie. "I can't stand on my own."

"What are you, a cripple?" taunted the smaller, red-haired boy.

"Shut up!" cried Janie. "I'm leaving!"

"You're not going anywhere, freak," said the brown-haired boy.

"Yeah, this is OUR hideout, freak," yelled the blond-haired boy. "Quick, grab her!"

The red-haired boy reached up and grabbed Janie's leg. As Janie held on tightly to my mane, I reared up with all of my strength, knocking the boy over. The brown-haired boy dropped my reins and fell backwards into the snow. I turned around and took off at a full gallop out of the woods, weaving around the trees. In the distance, I could hear the boys continue to shout hurtful names at Janie, who was holding on to my mane with all her strength. I could feel her tears soaking my neck.

Within moments, we were back at the paddock, where Heidi and Janie's mother were waiting, both frowning. Janie's mother pulled the sobbing girl from my back and held her close. Heidi took hold of my reins.

"Mom! Mom, get out here!" shouted Heidi up at the house.

A door opened and Mrs. Johnson raced out frantically.

"What's going on? Quick, let's get Janie inside," said Mrs. Johnson, urging Janie and her mother into the farmhouse. "Heidi, can you take Silver back to the stable?"

"Sure, Mom." said Heidi.

As Mrs. Johnson, Janie, and her mother went inside the house, Heidi led me towards the stable. I wanted to stay with Janie, though, so I started pulling Heidi towards the house again.

"Stop it, Silver!" commanded Heidi. "This is no time to get feisty."

I reared up against Heidi and she lost her grip. I took off galloping up the hill towards the house, reins flying at my side, as Heidi pursued me. I pressed my face up to each clear opening of the house, hoping to see my friend. Finally, as I peered in through the side opening, I could see Janie in her mother's arms, while Mrs. Johnson gave her something to dry her eyes.

Chapter 7

A Cold Spring

After several moments, Janie's tear soaked face noticed me in the window. She continued to sob. I had to do something, so I threw my head up, begging Janie to come to the window. Then I stepped away from the house and whinnied as loud as I could.

Janie and her mother watched me from the opening. Heidi had made it up the hill and was trying to catch me, but I kept weaving away from her. I started prancing around the yard in a circle, neighing and nickering at Janie. I tossed my head and arched my neck and tail gracefully. Mrs. Johnson's face soon appeared in the opening, and then I saw Janie's smiling face next to her!

Within moments, Janie's mother, with Janie in her arms, and Mrs. Johnson ran out to the yard. Janie held out her hand and I quickly snatched the apple inside. The little girl's tears had stopped and she pressed her warm face against mine.

"You're my best friend, Silver," Janie whispered. "I promise, you'll always be."

"I'll be sure to give you your favorite bran mash tonight, Silver!" said Mrs. Johnson, with a chuckle.

Later that evening, I told Pepper about the day's events.

"If I had known I would get a bran mash," said Pepper. "I would've jumped the fence and danced around too!"

"You would've never made it over the fence, Pepper," said Star, with a laugh.

"I agree..." I said.

"Say what you will." scolded Pepper. "But I still have a better chance at being the oldest living horse than either of you foals. Only twenty more years to go, I gather..."

The rest of the winter was peaceful and quiet. Pepper, Patches, and Star worked with many children. Since Janie was around so often, I was lucky enough to ride only with her. Soon, Mrs. Johnson had taken down the pine needle decorations off of her house. The orchard began to blossom with bright flowers, and the short apple trees grew buds. The field, once flooded with snow and ice, came alive with sweet green grass. I continued to gain weight and even earned myself a bigger girth size.

Along with the warmer weather came more children. Star and Patches took on the bigger workload, but Pepper was growing increasingly depressed. Mark hadn't been to see him since the snowfall ended.

"I know he's sick," said Pepper. "I'm afraid I'll never see him again. What's the point of being the oldest horse around if no one loves you?"

"Other children love you," said Patches. "They love your spots."

"I try never to get attached to one child," said Star, shaking her head. "That's why I don't mind that Janie and Silver are riding together. I like whoever I'm riding with and, when they stop, there's always another one to replace them."

"It's not the same," said the old Appaloosa.

One cloudy afternoon, Sarah started crying as she gave us our feed. Heidi ran over to her.

"What's the matter?" asked Heidi.

"Remember Mark? The little boy that loved Pepper?" sobbed Sarah. "I just got a call from his father. He passed away yesterday."

"Oh no! I didn't realize he was so sick. I thought he just stopped coming," said Heidi.

"His dad started crying on the phone, but he wanted us to know how happy Mark was when he was riding," Sarah continued, wiping tears from her cheeks. "He said we should never sell Pepper. He was Mark's best friend."

"I better go tell Mom. Will you come with me?" asked Heidi.

"Yeah, okay," said Sarah.

I looked over at Pepper, who was staring blankly out of his stall. I didn't know what to say to him and, before I could say anything, he was lying down in his bedding. Pepper would never be the same again.

Chapter 8

Pepper's Last Goodbye

Pepper's spirits went downhill once he heard of Mark's passing. Mrs. Johnson decided that it might be best to retire him, even just temporarily. I continued to work with Janie, and the other children took turns on Patches and Star. While we had our lessons in the paddock, Pepper stood alone in the field. Sometimes he grazed, but most of the time, he would just stand there, lost in his thoughts. He no longer joked with me as he used to, and the nights began to feel especially long for all of us.

As time went on, Mrs. Johnson noticed Pepper's condition getting even worse, so she thought a new rider might cheer him up. She was a sweet, red-headed girl named Stacy, but she couldn't help Pepper. Instead, he lost more weight and started tripping during his lessons since he was distracted. After that, Mrs. Johnson knew she couldn't use him for lessons anymore, and Stacy began riding Patches instead.

One morning, I woke up to find Pepper lying flat on his back, groaning loudly.

"What's wrong, Pep?" I asked.

"Ohhhh," groaned the old horse. "My stomach's bothering me, that's all. It'll pass."

It didn't pass. Pepper began rolling in his stall and Mrs. Johnson called in a veterinarian.

"Looks like a case of colic; very serious," said the vet. "I'll give him some painkillers, but unless we can get him to stand up, it doesn't look good."

Heidi and Sarah hugged each other and cried.

"What have you done to yourself?" I asked Pepper.

"Nothing," said the Appaloosa. "But frankly, if this is the end of me, I don't mind."

"How can you say that?" I shouted. "There's so much more that you could do here. Pull yourself together, there are other children that need you. You have to try!"

"It's too late for that," said Pepper. "I've been alive for a long time now. I helped Mark and lots of other kids. But you can't understand how I'm feeling, Silver. You're young. Until recently, you've never formed an attachment. But I can't play this game anymore. I'm tired of not knowing what's going to happen, and always ending up alone. I can't do it again."

Pepper blinked his eyes and fell asleep, but there was no way I could sleep that night. I stayed up and watched him, as Star and Patches drifted in and out.

The next morning, the veterinarian returned. He leaned over the old horse and checked him over. Pepper's groans had grown louder and more frequent. I wished there was some way that I could help him. Mrs. Johnson, Heidi, and Sarah all waited outside of Pepper's stall, with red, tear soaked faces.

"He's not getting any better," said the vet. "You could send him for surgery, but to be honest, it would be extremely risky for a horse his age. You might lose him halfway through the procedure. I hate to say this, but it might be best to put him out of his misery. I'm so sorry."

The three women cried loudly and hugged each other. Star's eyes grew wide and sad as she reached her head out of her stall to nuzzle Patches. Within a few moments, the old horse's groans had been silenced. While the vet said that Pepper had died from colic, I knew better. He had died from loneliness. Now, Pepper lay still, finally at peace.

Heidi and Sarah led Star and Patches to the field, but when Mrs. Johnson snapped on my leadrope, I fought her. I wanted to stay with Pepper as long as possible. I didn't want to leave him alone. Finally, she was able to pull me out of my stall, and I nickered back to the old Appaloosa. He didn't reply.

Star, Patches, and I couldn't even speak to one another that afternoon. We each wandered around the field, grazing quietly. At one point, I walked over to the brook where Pepper had always stood, and found his large hoofprints in the wet mud.

Suddenly, I heard loud hoofbeats coming from the paddock. Nothing was there. I'm sure it was Pepper and Mark, riding together once more, and whispering secrets to each other that no one else would ever hear.

Chapter 9

New Hope

The next morning, Janie was back and smiling at me as always. I was especially happy to see her since she was the only person who could take my mind off losing Pepper. Sarah was in the barn and walked over to greet Janie.

"Sarah, where's Pepper? I brought an extra treat for him," said Janie.

"Oh, Janie, we had to put him to sleep," said Sarah. "He was old and got sick."

"Oh no...I'm so, so sorry!" Janie said, lowering her head, and reaching out to give Sarah a hug. "He was such a great horse. I'll miss seeing him a lot."

"Thanks. He was always my favorite," said Sarah, her arms wrapped tight around Janie. "You can still ride Silver today, if you like."

That day, Janie rode better than ever. She told Sarah that she could feel my stomach with her legs more than before, even though she still couldn't move them. Sarah joked that it was because my belly was so big, but I knew better.

After our ride, Janie rolled alongside me in her wheelchair as I grazed in the orchard. I picked up the fallen apples and sweet grass as quickly as I could.

"Silver, you're going to be my horse," said Janie suddenly. "I'll ask Mom again today and she can't say no. I even worked out how I'll pay for board with Mrs. Johnson. This way, we'll always be together. You're all I talk about at school or with my friends. My art teacher even told me I had to stop drawing you, so I drew a brown horse instead."

I was so excited that I wanted to throw Janie on my back and race around. We gradually made our way back to the stable, where Janie's mother and Mrs. Johnson were waiting for us.

"So, it looks like you've got it all worked out," said Janie's mother.

"What? No, Mom, let me explain..." said Janie.

"He's yours," said her mother, then smiled as she handed some papers to Mrs. Johnson.

Janie hugged me with such force that I could barely breathe, then turned to her mother and did the same. While Mrs. Johnson was a great owner, I loved Janie more than anyone. From that point on, Janie came to visit me every day. Some days, Janie took care of barn chores, such as feeding us or cleaning tack, or grooming Star or Patches. She said it was in exchange for my board. But, as soon as she was finished, we'd either go for a ride or a walk outside together. The once quiet girl was now talkative and full of life, making friends with the new children that came to the farm and happy to tell me her deepest secrets.

"Don't tell my mom, or anyone yet, but I started writing stories about you, Silver!" said Janie, one summer afternoon. "I call them *The Adventures of Silver, the Wonder Horse*. In book one, an evil horse wrangler captures Star and Patches, and you show up to free them using your magic lasso! You can even fly! My English teacher thinks they're 'a work in progress.'"

While life went on at the farm, Pepper's stall remained empty. Heidi and Sarah had removed the stall's bedding and left a fan on during the day. Star thought a new horse would come, but by the time fall arrived, we had given up on the idea. Soon, Mrs. Johnson began leaving hay bales and bags of shavings in the stall instead, which made us all sad. I didn't know it then, but it would be years before the stall would be used for its former purpose.

Chapter 10

The Race

After becoming Janie's horse, I had the best care of my life. I was always well-kept by Mrs. Johnson, but she had several horses. Janie could spoil me completely. My coat was trimmed and neat and my whiskers were always kept short. My mane was never tangled. Once in a while, Janie would braid my mane and tail, making me feel like a real show pony. She would bring huge jars of oat treats and carrots every day, so I was never hungry.

When Janie wasn't around, I spent my time in the field with Star and Patches. My favorite days were when Janie let me run loose in the orchard, reading me one of her horse books or stories that she wrote about me.

"So Silver, I'm on book six now!" said Janie, during an evening in the orchard. "In this episode, you've mastered time travel, and are going to free cart horses that were mistreated in the 1800s. Pretty cool, huh?"

I nuzzled Janie and continued to eat the fallen apples. The taste of apples mixed with spring grass from the orchard was always irresistible to me.

On warmer days, Janie and I went trail riding in the woods with Heidi on Star and Sarah on Patches.

"Heidi, I've always wondered...where did Star originally come from?" asked Janie, on one of our trail rides.

"Oh, Star was a racehorse," said Heidi. "She won a couple of races, but then she was injured and moved on to low-level dressage competitions. Our mother's friend donated her to the farm a few years back and she settled right in."

"What about Patches?" asked Janie.

"Patches was used for pony rides at local parties or fairs," said Sarah. "He hated it. That's why I try to take him for trail rides as much as possible; walking around in a circle bores him. For whatever reason, he puts up with it here. I think the kids are much nicer to him, so he's more patient."

Later that fall, Mrs. Johnson had a party for all the kids. Star, Patches, and I took turns giving rides to different children. Afterwards, the children who were able to walk hopped around in large sacks, trying to race each other.

"See that, Silver," Janie said. "One day, I'm going to be able to do that."

"We're going to have some horse races now, everyone!" said Mrs. Johnson. "The first race will be at a walk, for anyone who needs some assistance. The second race will be at a trot, for anyone who can ride without a helper."

"Let's do the trotting race, Silver! I know we can win!" whispered Janie.

Janie and I waited on the outside of the paddock while the walking race began. Star's huge stride won her the race easily, and Tom, the little boy riding with her, was practically jumping out of the saddle with joy. Star was rewarded with a huge apple. My mouth began to water. I knew the trotting race was ours.

Star was also entered in the trotting race, with a girl named Susie, and Patches raced again with a boy named Dominic. The three of us were lined against the paddock fence. I pawed at the ground, imagining the juicy apple I would win, and the smile on Janie's face. Janie took a tight hold of my mane. A whistle rang out, and we were off!

Janie held herself up as her legs bounced off of my sides. She clucked and urged me into a fast trot. We were in front! Star was right behind me, and I could hear Patches making his way closer. I picked up speed as Janie touched the far fence and we turned around, heading for the finish line.

Star took the lead and I snorted with anger. I dug into the dirt and saw Star's long neck hanging out in front. I picked up my pace and stuck out my short neck as far as I could, and my muzzle crossed the wire first! We won!

Janie reached forward, gave me a big kiss, and wrapped her arms around my neck. Mrs. Johnson ran over to present me with my treat, as Star looked my way and pawed at the ground, kicking dirt in my direction.

"How did you do that? I was a racehorse! You're half my size!" said Star, disgusted.

"I wanted Janie to win," I said. "That's enough inspiration to make me beat anyone."

Chapter 11

Changes

Time passed at Meadow Brook Farm as quickly as the wind through the apple trees. Janie grew taller and more beautiful with each passing year, as I grew older and wider. Both Heidi and Sarah had left the farm, leaving Mrs. Johnson alone in the house. Due to developing arthritis, Star was now retired, but her favorite former rider, Billy, would visit her every now and again. Stacy, the girl who had started her lessons on Pepper years ago, had since bought Patches for her own horse, but kept him on the farm and used him for lessons. There were only a few disabled kids who rode these days, so one pony was enough. And I was happy being with Janie and my friends.

Janie had turned fifteen that summer, and I was a mature fourteen in human years. As Janie's weak legs grew, she could actually reach the ground as she sat on me. One day, during our usual walk in the orchard, Janie confided in me:

"Some friends have invited me on a trip," Janie said. "I'm leaving in a few weeks, and I'll be gone for about a month. Don't worry, Mrs. Johnson will groom you everyday, and maybe have you do a lesson or two, so you won't get bored. I'll be back before you know it. This time, I'll have some of my own adventures to tell the wonder horse."

A trip? For seven years now, I was used to seeing Janie several times a week. I knew I would miss her terribly, but at least I had Star and Patches for company. Janie said "goodbye for now," as she filled up a bucket with carrots and apples in the field. She wheeled off and I whinnied for her as the car roared away.

For a while, I wasn't ridden. I didn't mind the break. Star, Patches, and I roamed the field every day. Then, one morning, a little blond-haired girl raced into the stable. She looked into every stall, her purple coverings reminiscent of Janie as a young girl. The green-eyed girl walked up to my stall and presented me with a carrot. Not a bad way to make an introduction.

"S-I-L-V-E-R," she spelled, slowly. "Silvaaar, oh yeah, Silver! You're the pony I'm supposed to ride today! I'm Christina. You know my sister, Stacy. Mom says I'm finally old enough to ride with her today."

I curiously sniffed the little girl as Mrs. Johnson led me from my stall. Mrs. Johnson helped Christina brush and tack me up. When we were finished, Christina led me outside, where Stacy and Patches were waiting.

"There he is," said Stacy. "You'll love him. Janie tells me he is a great beginner horse."

"I hope so," said Christina. "I've never ridden a horse before."

Patches and I rode down the stone path towards the trail together. It was very hot that day, so even at a walk we were sweating. Luckily, it was cooler once we were in the forest, sheltered by the pine trees from above. While the ride was peaceful, I couldn't help but miss my Janie. I wondered what she was doing, and if she missed me too.

Days passed, one after the other. But one morning, as I enjoyed the new sprouts of grass in our field, a familiar voice caught my attention. I pricked up my ears and squinted as I looked towards the fence. There was a tall girl in a wheelchair rolling toward the gate.

"Silver! How is my boy doin'?" said the soft voice.

Before the red-haired girl could even swing the gate open, I picked up a canter and raced to the fenceline. Janie hugged me, then patted my head.

"Did you miss me, boy?" she asked.

I nickered softly and nuzzled her warm face. I never wanted to be without her again.

As summer ended, I thought life would return to normal. Instead, Janie no longer took me for long walks in the orchard, or trail rides. She seemed to enjoy my company, but now she would come to finish her chores and spend less time with me. Pepper's voice echoed in my mind again:

"They went away. Like all children do."

Was Janie going to leave me? She always promised me that I would never be sold, but as time wore on, she saw me less and less. I was starting to know how Pepper felt all those years ago.

"You know she loves you, Silver," said Star, reassuringly. "Maybe she's just busy. Teenagers are like that."

I wanted to believe her, but soon, Janie stopped coming to the farm all together.

Chapter 12

A Disease Called Loneliness

As time without Janie went on, I felt sicker and sicker. I began to cough loudly and strange liquid leaked from my nostrils. One afternoon, after I couldn't eat a bite of my grain, Mrs. Johnson called the vet. After he looked me over, the vet knew immediately what it was.

"Equine influenza," he said. "It's highly contagious, so we'll need to quarantine Silver immediately."

"We have another small barn that we use for storage," Mrs. Johnson responded. "It's dark, but we can clean it out quickly and put him in there."

In the afternoon, Mrs. Johnson led me to the small barn, which was adjacent to the riding paddock. It was pitch black and cramped. Despite not being as small, it reminded me of the old shed that my former owner had locked me in. Mrs. Johnson filled the barn with hay and water and then left me in the darkness. My entire body ached and I was so tired that I had to lie down and sleep.

When I finally woke up, it felt like I had slept for days. Suddenly, the barn door creaked open and a stream of dim sunlight poked through. There was Janie! She wheeled up to me and threw herself onto the hay-covered ground. As Janie felt my warm body, she suddenly began to cry.

"Oh Silver! I'm so, so sorry," she said, with tears racing down her pale face. "If I had been here to take care of you, this may never have happened. I promise, I'll never leave you alone for so long again."

She kissed my soft head and sang to me, as she did as a child:

"Silver is the best-est horse...the great-est hooorse there ever was!"

It was then that Janie first tried to stand on her own. She climbed back into the chair, then turned and put both of her arms firmly on the handles, lifting herself up. Janie wobbled for a moment and stood tall.

"Look, Silver!" she cheered. "I'm st..."

But suddenly, she fell back down.

"It was worth a shot," said Janie, discouraged. "But right now, all I care about is getting you well. That's all that matters to me."

Chapter 13

From Little Girl to Grown-Up

I gradually returned to full strength and soon Janie and I were taking walks in the orchard again. Many times, she would sit with me and jot down the stories she had told me as a child. Other days, she would read to me about colleges that she hoped to attend after high school.

"I can't wait to go to college!" Janie said. "It's going to be so exciting!"

I didn't understand what college was exactly, but I knew it sounded like a far away place. I wondered if Janie would leave me behind.

One day in the field, I brought up my concerns to Star and Patches.

"I hope I never have to leave this place, and both of you," I said. "I mean, if Janie goes to this college place…"

"Wait," Star said. "I've heard this sob story before, but from an old Appaloosa's mouth. You worry too much, Silver. What ever happened to the pony who was so grateful for the slightest bit of attention? Janie loves you as much as she ever did. You're a large part of her life. If she moves, I'm sure you'll go with her."

"We'll miss you, if that happens," said Patches. "I mean, you're not bad, for a peewee."

"I bet you can't catch this peewee…" I said, with a laugh.

I took off at a full gallop, with Star and Patches in hot pursuit. We kicked up our heels and extended our legs in perfect harmony, side by side. Janie may have been my best human friend, but I couldn't have asked for any better companions than Star and Patches.

After a mild winter, spring arrived, but with it came more problems. For years now, Mrs. Johnson was giving lessons to less and less children, and Heidi and Sarah weren't around to help. Mrs. Johnson would spend less time in the stables, and more time up in her house. Now she hardly smiled and seemed more anxious than ever. Then, one morning, as Janie groomed me in my stall, Mrs. Johnson came into the stable with a stocky, gray-haired man.

"You must have some horses for sale. What about this one?" asked the man.

"Oh, this is Star," said Mrs. Johnson. "I really think she's past work, though. She's got a bit of a swayback and arthritis now. The other two horses are privately owned."

"I'll offer you $1,000," the man said. "My eight year-old needs a calm horse, and this one seems perfect. Nice and docile."

Star tried to nip the man, but he pushed her away.

"I'll really have to think it over," said Mrs. Johnson.

"Alright, but don't wait too long," said the man, as he left the stable. "From what I hear, you'll be out of business in a month."

Janie wheeled out of my stall and over to Mrs. Johnson.

"You can't sell Star, Mrs. Johnson," Janie pleaded. "She's too old. What if they overwork her? You owe her a good retirement."

"I..." Mrs. Johnson hesitated. "I can't even pay the mortgage, Janie. I don't know how I can afford to keep Star. I didn't want to tell you this yet, but I might have to sell the farm. It's just too expensive and we don't give enough lessons these days."

"You can't!" shouted Janie. "I'll help you. I've been taking marketing and journalism courses in high school. I can make flyers and start a website. We'll get kids to come back here. You'll see, it'll work!"

Janie did as she had promised. Many days, she would rush in to spend time with me, and then head off to help Mrs. Johnson. She would often say:

"Silver, I love you, but I have to save the farm. I'll be back after I drop off these flyers and brochures!"

The next day, Janie showed me her brochures.

"See, Silver, that's a picture of you and me on the cover," said Janie. "You must have been about eight there. Now, you're the official Meadow Brook mascot. Mom and I spent all day dropping these off at tack stores and telling people there about the farm. Tomorrow I'm going to a horse show with Stacy. The people running the show even gave us a free booth. I hope it's enough to help Mrs. Johnson."

All of Janie's work eventually paid off. By midsummer, Meadow Brook Farm was once again overrun with little children. We were so busy that one horse wasn't enough, so Janie would have me do a few lessons a week to help Patches out. It was nice working with other children and seeing their smiles after they took their first ride.

One warm afternoon, a few of Janie's friends decorated the stable for her sixteenth birthday. One of the girls put a silly hat on me and Janie nearly fell over with laughter when she entered my stall. Mrs. Johnson suggested they take Patches and me into the riding paddock for some pony rides, which all the girls loved, even though they could literally stretch their legs to the ground from our backs. But the biggest surprise was yet to come.

On our way back to the stable, I noticed Mrs. Johnson sitting quietly under one of the apple trees. Suddenly, a long, light bay face raised its head and stared at us. He was tall and broad, with a white stripe on his face. He nickered kindly to me as Janie wheeled over to Mrs. Johnson.

"Who's this? A new lesson horse?" asked Janie.

"Not quite," said Mrs. Johnson, with a chuckle.

"Surprise! Happy Birthday, Janie!" shouted Janie's friends, along with her mother and Mrs. Johnson.

"We all chipped in and found you the perfect Quarter horse!" said Mrs. Johnson. "His old owners called him Brownie. He's only five years old and such a sweetie. We thought it was about time you had a larger horse."

"Thank you all so much!" shouted Janie. "But, I can't possibly sell Silver. I don't think I could afford two horses. How much would board be for both of them?"

"Nothing at all," said Mrs. Johnson. "If it wasn't for your help, I would've lost the farm. Now business is thriving. As long as you continue to help out, they can both stay for free. If you'd like to offer either of them for lessons once in a while, that would be great."

"We really want you to have him, Janie," said her mother. "You've earned it."

"Of course, I'll keep him!" said Janie. "I'm sure Silver will love him!"

I wasn't so sure. Suddenly, there was this handsome, younger horse for Janie to love and spend time with. He moved into Pepper's old stall, but I barely said a word to him for days. I even avoided him in the field. Janie would come see us every day, spending some time with him, and some with me, riding one of us each day. I couldn't hide my jealousy and I wished for life to return to the way it was, as Janie's only equine friend.

Chapter 14

Brownie

One morning, after I had finished my grain, Brownie spoke to me.

"You're going to have to give up on ignoring me sometime," said the bay horse.

"It's worked so far," I replied.

"Yes, but it's not like you have anything to be jealous about," Brownie said. "If anything, I should be jealous of you. Janie loves you! Every day, when we go trail riding, she tells me stories about you. Like that time in the woods when you saved her from those boys. Or when you won the race together. Sounds like you're the best of friends. You'll always be her favorite, and I'm fine with that."

"Really?" I asked. "I was hoping Janie still felt that way. I'm sorry. I didn't know how to react to you. Janie and I have been alone for all these years, but I guess there's no reason why we can't share her."

"Thanks," Brownie said. "I'm glad, because Janie's great, and I know if you weren't happy, she'd give me away immediately."

"I'm sure that won't happen," I said. "So, now that we're finally on speaking terms, where are you from, Brownie?"

Brownie closed his deep brown eyes and sighed.

"Well, I grew up in Kentucky, on a farm with other Quarter horses," he said. "Most of them were show horses, but they didn't think I was bold or flashy enough to compete more than a few times. I was eventually sold to a woman who thought I'd make a good jumper, but all I did was knock the rails down."

"That's not good..." I said, with a laugh. "Did you like being a show horse, while it lasted?"

"Not really," the bay horse continued. "I prefer not having to travel around in a trailer. All I ever wanted was a nice owner and some good friends. I like Janie a lot and I hope she never sells me."

"Same here," I said.

"There's no way she ever would," said Brownie. "Janie told me that you've been her only freedom since she was little. You're a part of her now."

Chapter 15

Where I Belong

Before I knew it, Janie was in her last year of high school. Brownie and I were always excited to hear about which colleges Janie had heard from. We learned college was a place for humans to continue learning as adults. Mrs. Johnson was busy with lessons, so Brownie and I helped out. Her daughter, Sarah, was now a physical therapist, so she moved back into the farmhouse to help with the lessons. We rarely saw Heidi, but when we did, she was always sure to stop by and make us each a bran mash.

As for Star, her longtime friend, Billy, had moved away, but she remained in great shape for a horse nearly thirty years old.

"Pepper would hate it if I outlived the oldest known horse, wouldn't he?" said Star. "I think I might just do that..."

Patches' days were still packed with lessons and playing with Christina, since Stacy was away at college most of the time.

"I don't care what happens to me from here on," said Patches. "No matter how bad things get, I can always think of the fun I've had with these girls."

I had been with Janie for ten wonderful years. Ten years of laughs, games, tears, and special secrets, which I'll never tell anyone. Except for *The Adventures of Silver the Wonder Horse*, of course...

One day that winter, Janie came rolling into the barn proudly, her hands hurriedly rolling over her wheelchair's tires.

"Look at this, boys!" Janie shouted, holding a thin piece of paper. "I got into my first choice, Ashton University in North Carolina! You guys are going to love it there! Mom and I took a trip and there's nothing but grass and trees wherever you look. It's real horse country, if you ask me. I'll be living in a dorm—I can't wait to find out who my roommate is. I'm going to board you two nearby, and I think they'll even give me a huge discount if Brownie becomes part of the equestrian team! I'll be right back...I need to show Mrs. Johnson the acceptance letter!"

Star and Patches looked at me with sunken eyes.

"North Carolina?" said Brownie. "It sounds familiar. I think I had a show there, once. If I remember correctly, it's very pretty, but far away."

"I don't want to see it..." I said. "I love Janie, but my home is still here, in the orchard, or along the brook, or under the pine trees...with all of you!"

"Silver," said Star. "You said yourself that home was wherever Janie is. You'll be happy anywhere with her."

"I know I said that. But, what happens if I never see either of you again?"

"I don't know about you," interrupted Patches. "But I'd rather be with someone caring like Janie than on the same farm all of my life. You've been without Janie here before and you were miserable. She is what's important."

Patches and Star were right. Janie was my past, present, and future. It was sad to know that I would be leaving my friends, and I never dreamed that I would have to say goodbye to them like this. But somehow, I knew they would always be with me.

Chapter 16

A Final Farewell

I spent every moment I could in our field, sharing stories with Star and Patches. I would miss them more than anything. I would also miss the sparrows and crows singing loudly overhead, and the sound of a happy child riding. The children who couldn't walk had always been the most special to me; more than one of them said that riding me felt like flying. I would miss the apples in the orchard, where Janie always told me stories. I would even miss the large farmhouse, where Mrs. Johnson stood on the porch, watching us run in the field.

A few days before leaving, Janie took me for one last walk in the orchard. It was raining lightly, making the grass slippery. We went along slowly, but as Janie pushed the wheels to go down the hill, her wheelchair skidded downward and tumbled over. Janie landed on the soggy grass and I ran to her side. She looked at the wheelchair, now covered in mud, and slowly eased herself up. After pulling herself to her knees, her hands slid in the wet grass and she fell.

"That's it; I'm going to do it this time!" Janie said. "Silver, come help me!"

I moved closer to Janie's side and she grabbed my neck and mane for support. She pulled herself up and then fell again. Janie let out a deep breath and grunted. Her face was contorted. I couldn't stand seeing her in pain.

"Owww…" Janie cried. "Silver, don't move, just give me a minute."

Janie wrapped her arms completely around my neck, pulling on me to lift herself into an upright position. Her breath quickened and gripe tightened. I didn't budge, my hooves firmly planted for Janie's support. This time, her crooked legs fully straightened; she was standing!

"Silver! Is this really happening?" Janie shouted, her face red and covered with tears.

I couldn't believe my eyes. Like a newborn foal, Janie took one wobbly step forward, gasping from discomfort, then leaned back against me. Despite the pain, Janie's face lit up with joy. Suddenly, two shadowy figures raced towards us.

"Janie, are you all right?" shouted Sarah.

"I'm fine, just fine! Look!" said Janie. "I'm up!"

Janie took another fragile step away from me before losing her balance. She grabbed my neck again and I held her steady. Mrs. Johnson hugged Janie tightly and all three women screamed in amazement.

"See, Silver!" Janie shouted. "I told you that someday I would walk, using my own legs!"

I nuzzled her face and hair, the two of us covered in mud. For the first time, Janie was able to look down at me, without sitting on my back. It was the most beautiful thing I'd ever seen; Janie standing tall, widely smiling against the dark clouds above her. After ten years of hoping, this moment had seemed impossible, until now.

A few days later, Janie returned. It was time for us to move. Mrs. Johnson hugged Janie, then loaded Brownie and me into a large trailer. Brownie went first. I stopped on the ramp and neighed goodbye towards the field.

"Don't forget us!" shouted Star and Patches.

"How could I ever forget my friends?" I called back, then walked onto the trailer.

As the trailer pulled away, I screamed out:

"Star, don't forget—you've still got to beat the age record!"

The last thing I saw at Meadow Brook Farm was the bright bay mare and the pinto gelding racing after us along the fenceline.

While I still miss my friends, life in North Carolina has been peaceful. Janie is now in her third year of school and can walk slowly with braces and a cane. She constantly tells me that soon she'll need no help at all. I am now retired for the most part and spend my days with Brownie, who is as fat and happy as I am. But once in a while, in my dreams, I still return to Meadow Brook Farm, back to the days when I was a shy pony and Janie's New Legs.

Made in the USA
Middletown, DE
25 April 2022

64712159R00031